ALPACA PATI'S FANCY FLEECE

by Tracey Kyle

Illustrations by Yoss Sanchez

RP|KIDS
PHILADELPHIA

Running Press Kids
Hachette Book Group
1290 Avenue of the Americas, New York, NY 10104
www.runningpress.com/rpkids
@RP_Kids

Printed in China

First Edition: September 2019

Published by Running Press Kids, an imprint of Perseus Books, LLC, a subsidiary of Hachette Book Group, Inc. The Running Press Kids name and logo is a trademark of the Hachette Book Group.

The Hachette Speakers Bureau provides a wide range of authors for speaking events. To find out more, go to www.hachettespeakersbureau.com or call (866) 376-6591.

The publisher is not responsible for websites (or their content) that are not owned by the publisher.

Print book cover and interior design by Christopher Eads.

Library of Congress Control Number: 2018963236

ISBNs: 978-0-7624-9414-9 (hardcover), 978-0-7624-9467-5 (ebook), 978-0-7624-9413-2 (ebook), 978-0-7624-9496-5 (ebook)

1010

10 9 8 7 6 5 4 3 2 1

FOR MY SISTER-IN-LAW, PATTY EPPS
-T.K.

FOR EDUARDO
-Y.S.

High up in the Andes, on a mountain in Peru,
Pati the alpaca gussied up for her debut.

Mami fluffed her downy fur
and tied a beaded bow.

"Find your *cría* friends at school.
There now off you go!"

All the young alpacas met for class beside a lake,
and when they spotted Pati, they did a doubletake.

"Pati," her *amigas* hummed, "your fleece is soft and sleek!"
And that's the moment Pati the alpaca felt unique.

Every morning Pati chose adornments for her fur, dazzling her alpaca friends and causing quite a stir.

Velvet bows.

Sparkly clips.

Headbands lined with flowers.

Pati's morning prep became
a drama taking hours.

At the lake, she loved to sneak a peek at her reflection, cherishing her fine *piel* and noting its perfection.

One day, *cría* Carmen whispered, "Pati, *¡no te creas!*

In the spring we lose our fur and then we'll all be *feas!"*

Pati stumbled home to Mami.
"Tell me! Is it true?"

Pati cried. Mami sighed.
"It's what the farmers do."

Sprinting down the mountain roads,
she came upon the city,
desperate not to go back home
and lose what made her pretty.

Pati shuffled through the streets,
flustered and fatigued.

And then . . . she saw a market.
Pati stopped. She was intrigued.

El mercado overflowed with heaps of handmade goods:
Flowy ponchos, cozy *guantes, suéteres* with hoods.

Soft *bufandas*. Knitted socks.
Rows of *zapatillas*.

Heavy blankets perfect for
the mountains' *noches frías*.

Multi-colored *bolsos* next to *gorros* and *abrigos*,
waiting to be purchased by a crop of new *amigos*.

Pati touched the merchandise, studying each piece.
Every single one was made with pure alpaca fleece.

Fleece that had been spun, then dyed,
then woven, cut, and sewn.

Fleece that all the villagers were
proud to buy and own.

Suddenly, she understood.
The *pueblo* needed wool.

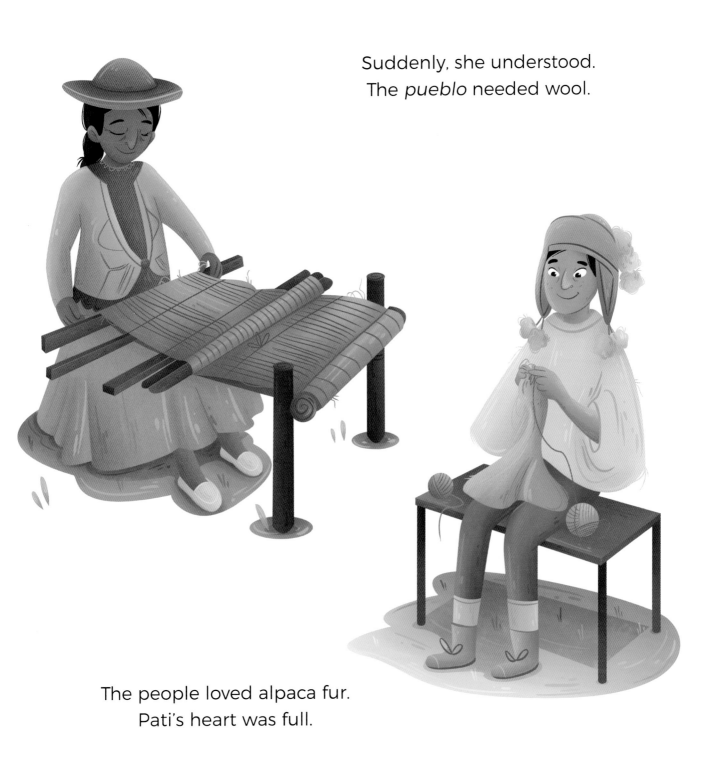

The people loved alpaca fur.
Pati's heart was full.

In the spring, when mountain farmers
came to do the shearing,

Pati led the herd and was the first one volunteering.

Mami beamed with pride and smiled, "Here's your beaded bow.
Wear it as a necklace since the fur takes time to grow."

Spring turned into summer on the mountain in Peru.
By autumn, Pati's fleece had sprouted, silky-soft and new.

Fall turned into winter, and one night there was a storm.
But Pati knew the people in the *pueblo* would be warm.

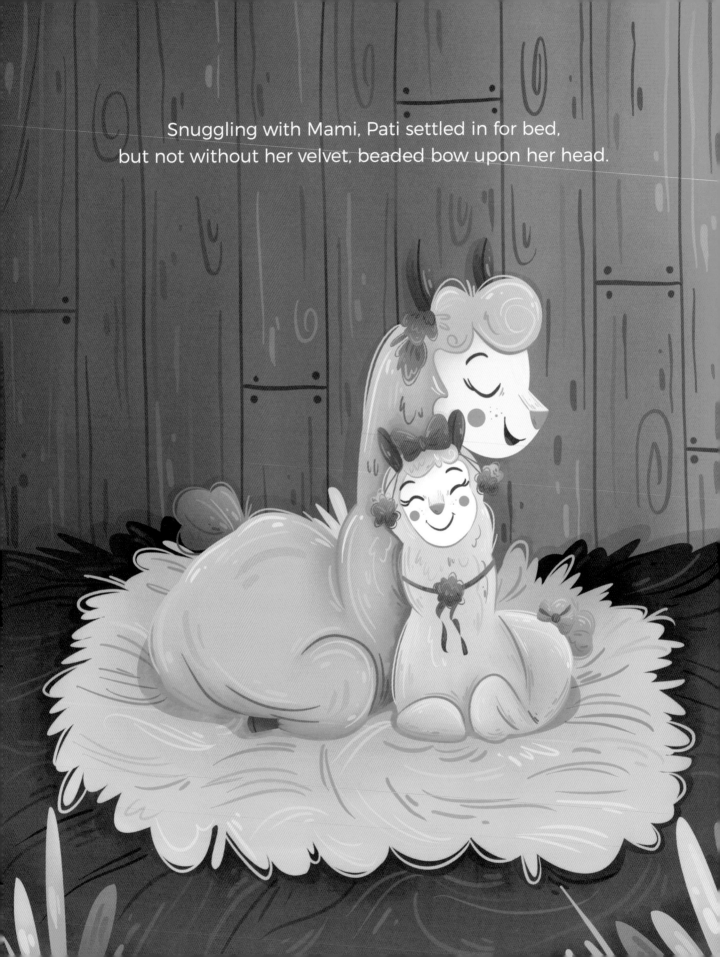

Snuggling with Mami, Pati settled in for bed,
but not without her velvet, beaded bow upon her head.

GLOSSARY

(words are listed in order of appearance)

cría	a baby alpaca	CREE-ah
amigas/ amigos	friends	Ah-MEE-gahs/ Ah-MEE-gohs
piel	fur	Pee-EHL
¡No te creas!	Don't think so much of yourself!	NO TAY CRAY-ahs
feas	ugly	FAY-ahs
el mercado	market	Ehl mehr-KAH-doh
suéteres	sweaters	SWEH-teh-rehs
guantes	gloves	GWAHN-tehs
bufandas	scarves	boo-FAHN-dahs
zapatillas	slippers	Sah-pah-TEE-yas
noches frías	cold nights	NOH-chehs-FREE-yas
bolsos	purses	BOHL-sohs
gorros	hats	GOH-rrhos
abrigos	coats	Ah-BREE-gohs
pueblo	town	PWEH-bloh

AUTHOR'S NOTE

The Andes mountain range is the longest in the world, stretching about 4,400 miles from the south of Argentina and Chile to the north of Colombia, taking in parts of Peru, Bolivia, and Ecuador. In the *altiplano*, or high plateau, of the mountains in Peru and Bolivia, lives a very valuable animal in South America—the alpaca. Smaller than its cousin, the llama, alpacas are prized for their unique fur.

There are only two types of alpaca breeds. Suri alpacas have long, wavy hair that hangs like dreadlocks, and huacaya (wuh-kai-ya) alpacas have shorter, fluffier hair. Alpaca wool is strong, soft, and warm, much softer and warmer than the wool from sheep. It is also resistant to rain and snow.

I visited an alpaca farm in Virginia, where I live, and was amazed watching these adorable, playful animals hold their heads high and trot proudly and purposefully. It was nearly 100 degrees when I met them, and they would only leave the shade of their barn when the farmer took out a hose to give them a cool bath! Here, I learned that alpacas do not like to be shorn and need to be held down for the process. From this experience, *Alpaca Pati* was born.

TEN ALPACA FUN FACTS

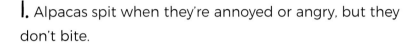

1. Alpacas spit when they're annoyed or angry, but they don't bite.

2. Alpaca fleece is hypoallergenic, meaning you can't be allergic to it.

3. Alpacas come in 22 different colors, from white to tan to black.

4. Alpacas make a humming sound to express most emotions, but they shriek when they're angry!

5. Alpacas are sheared in the spring and produce between five and ten pounds of wool.

6. Alpaca wool was so prized by the Incas that only royalty could wear it.

7. Alpacas can live to be between 15 and 20 years old.

8. Alpacas, like llamas, are part of the camel family.

9. Alpacas eat mostly grass.

10. Alpacas like to hang out together, and even use the same area as a bathroom!